To my Nephew Max, thank you for inspiring this journey.

Text copyright © Chrissy Metge 2020

The moral rights of author and illustrator
have been asserted, this book is copyright.

Illustrations by Dmitry Chizhov

www.chrissymetge.com
www.ducklingpublishing.com

A catalogue record for this book is available from
the National Library of New Zealand.

ISBN - 978-0-473-54634-2

Duckling
publishing

Table of Contents

4

Max

By
Chrissy Metge

Illustrated
by Dmitry Chizhov

And his Big Imagination
The Beach

"Let's go to the beach today," Mother says.
"Hooray," says Max. "I can't wait to see what adventures we will have."

6

Mother and Max arrive at the beach. Colorful umbrellas stretch as far as the eye can see. The hot summer sun beats down. "Let's make a sand castle," Max says. He gets out his shiny new bucket and spade.

Bucket by bucket, golden sand piles high.
Mother and Max make a sand dragon
with a long scary tail. It breathes fire
made with seaweed from the seashore.
"Wow!" says Max. He climbs on top of
the sand dragon's back. "He's a giant!"

Suddenly, the sand dragon comes alive! He shakes his giant head and
looks at Max. "You better hold on tight," he says with a big toothy grin.
With a mighty leap, the dragon jumps upward into the air.
Soon Max is flying up high in the sky with the beach far below.

9

The dragon dives down, down to the
sea below. Max hangs onto his back
tightly as, they zip through the waves
that are making Giant Barrel rolls.

Flip. Flop. Splash. Dolphins jump out of the water,
greeting their friends with clever fun tricks.

10

A huge tail pops out of the sea. A whale wants to play too.
His blowhole spurts water high into the air.
All of a sudden an enormous wave races toward them.
It hits Max and the dragon! Max takes a gasp...

Thump!

Max opens his eyes as he hits the sand.
He has fallen off the sand dragon's back.
Mother looks at Max and smiles. "It's time to go," she says.
"Did you have fun on your sand adventure?"

"Oh, yes," Max replies. "The sand dragon was wonderful.
Next time I want to make a sand whale, too!"
Leaving the beach, Max looks at the sea once more.
A whale flips his tail to say goodbye. Max smiles and waves.
"See you next time!" he says.

Max

And his Big Imagination
The Safari

by
Chrissy Metge

illustrated by
Dmitry Chizov

"*Aaachoo! Aaachoo!*" Max doesn't feel well. His nose drips water everywhere. "You have a cold," says Mother. "Stay inside today." Max nods his head. "I will play with my toys in my room."

Max pulls out his explorer's hat and puts it on his head. Then opening his toy box, he takes out his safari animals and spreads them all over the floor. "*Aaaachooooo!*" Max's sneeze sounds just like an elephant!

17

Suddenly, Max is in Africa.

He is on a real safari!

In front of him, a herd of elephants drink from a watering hole.

The biggest elephant raises his wrinkly grey trunk at Max and smiles.

"Would you like a ride?" he asks.

"Yes, please," says Max. His heart beats fast with excitement.

The elephant coils his enormous trunk around Max's stomach. Then he lifts Max high into the air and onto his back.

Max looks around wide-eyed.

He sees wildlife everywhere. Giraffes, antelopes, zebras, and lions…

A giraffe stretches her long neck far up into a tree. Munch, munch, crunch. Max laughs as he watches the giraffe enjoy her meal.

All of a sudden, Max hears

a thunderous sound!

The ground begins to shake. "What is happening?" says Max.
The elephants don't know. They huddle together while the ground
shakes, rumbles and grumbles.

"Hold on!" says the elephant. "It's the buffalo!"

Coming over the horizon, a herd of buffalo
thunders past Max and the elephants.

A big dust cloud follows behind, covering everything. "*Aaachooo*!"
Max sneezes again. When he opens his eyes he is back in his room
wearing his explorer's hat.

"That was a loud sneeze, Max," says Mother. She tousles his hair and smiles. "Yes," says Max. "But not as loud as a herd of buffalo!"

Max looks down at his toys. An elephant raises his trunk to wave goodbye. Max waves back. He can hardly wait for his next adventure.

23

Max

And his Big Imagination

Written by
Chrissy Metge

The Sandpit

Illustrated by
Dmitry Chizhov

On a beautiful sunny day, Max and Mother are outside having a picnic. Mother is relaxing and reading a book, while Max is playing in his sandpit. "***Brrrrrrrrm. Brrrrrrm,***" Max yells as he operates his big digger through the sand.

"Here, Max," Mother says as she hands him his construction helmet.

"Happy digging!" "Thanks, Mother," Max says as he puts the hat on.

Suddenly, Max is driving a real digger in a giant quarry.

He notices trucks moving around piles of stones and dirt.

Max lurches his digger forward. There is a big boulder in front of a high cliff that needs to move . *"Brrmmm. Brrmmmm. Brrm."*

Smoke pumps out as the digger strains to pick up the huge rock. Its large tires turn slowly, and eventually the boulder moves aside. "Wow!" says Max as he looks at what was behind the boulder. Imbedded into the cliff is a huge skeleton of a Tyrannosaurus Rex!

The cliff starts to **RUMBLE** and **SHAKE**.

Max watches as rocks stream down,
and suddenly the dinosaur's head
detaches from the cliff.

"Hello, Max," the dinosaur says.

"Thank you for moving that boulder.
It's been in my way for a long time."

30

"Max, will you help some of my friends?"

"Sure," Max says excitedly. Max zooms his digger around the quarry,

helping to release more of the dinosaur skeletons. Soon he is surrounded

by a Stegosaurus, Brachiosaurus, and a Triceratops.

"Thank you Max for setting us free," They say.

Max smiles. But then he looks up at the sky. Dark clouds loom overhead and the skies open with rain.

Max finds himself suddenly back in his sandpit
with raindrops coming down

"Come on, Max," says Mother as she gathers
up their things. "We better get inside."

Max reaches for his digger and sees a huge hole with a little toy dinosaur
at the bottom. The dinosaur winks at Max, and Max winks back. He can
hardly wait for his next adventure.

Max
And his Big Imagination

By
Chrissy Metge

The Race Car

Illustrated by
Dmitry Chizhov

"Wow!" Max says as he looks at the huge empty box in the middle of the lounge. He just woke up and is still in his pajamas. "Morning, Max," Mother says. "The box is yours to play with. You can make it into anything you want."

"Hooray!" Max shouts as he jumps in and gets to work. With Mother's help, the box takes shape in no time. "Yay! It's done!" Max says.

"Well done," says Mother.

"It's a great racing car!"

Mother hands Max his bike helmet. "This will help with your race," she says.

Max puts on his helmet and finds himself on a giant racetrack.

The clock is counting down. *3... 2... 1... GO!*

ZOOOOOOOM!

The other cars immediately take off. Max quickly puts his foot down
on the pedal, but the gear is in reverse and Max takes off backwards!
He quickly turns the car around, his wheels burning rubber.

"GOOOOOOOOOO, MAXXXX!" the crowd shouts. Max zooms off in a cloud of smoke, hot on the trail of the other cars.

Max is in hot pursuit. He is in second place! All of a sudden his car starts to slow as the petrol light starts blinking! "Oh, no!" Max yells.

He is suddenly back in his lounge as Mother comes in with breakfast.

"It's time for breakfast, Max," Mother says. "You need fuel to keep going.

You can keep playing when you have finished." "Yes," Max says excitedly.

"And I will win the race next time!"

Max
And his Big Imagination

The Shadow

By
Chrissy Metge

Illustrated by
Dmitry Chizhov

Mother and Max are walking back from the park on a sunny afternoon with their dog, Hugo. "What's that, Mother?" Max asks in a scared voice.

He points to a dark shape on the ground.

"Don't be afraid, Max," Mother says.

"Those are our shadows."

"No," Max says. "It's a big tiger!"

He puts his hands over his eyes,

hoping the tiger will go away.

47

"GRRROOOOOWWWLLLLLL!"

Max opens his eyes. A huge tiger is standing before him!

But before he can run away, three tiger cubs jump on him, licking his face!

"Hello, Max," Mother Tiger says. "I'm sorry if I scared you."

"It's okay," Max says. "I think shadows are scarier!"

"Shadows can be lots of fun," Mother Tiger says.

"Would you like to join us? We were just about to play Catch the Shadow."

"Sure!" Max says excitedly.

The cubs race off, with Max and Mother Tiger behind them. Soon they come to a big shady area surrounded by huge leafy trees.

50

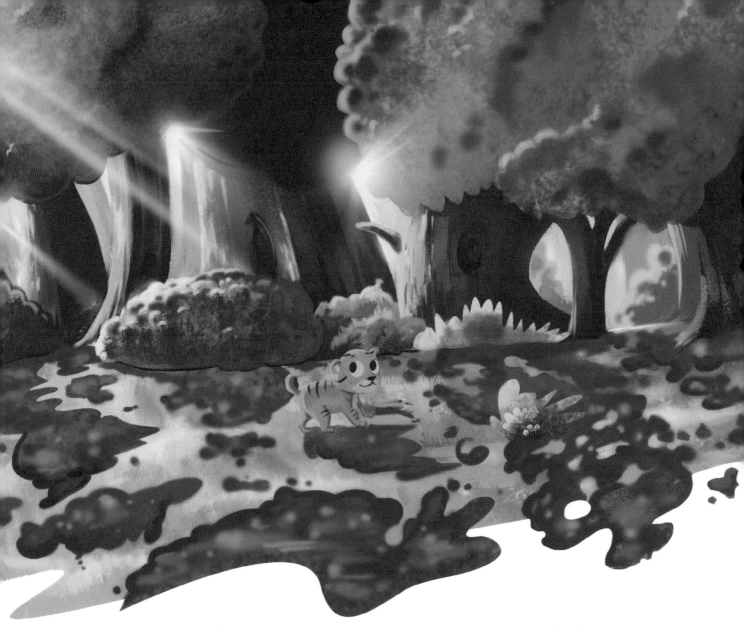

The sun is streaming through the trees, making shadows of all shapes and sizes on the ground. It is a little windy, and the shadows seem to be moving around.

The cubs are already jumping from shadow to shadow, trying to land on one before the shadow races off. "Your turn, Max," Mother Tiger says.

Max sees a shadow that looks like a monkey swinging from branch to branch. He quickly runs and jumps on it. "Ha ha! I got the monkey," he shouts. The shadow jumps again, and he runs to catch it.

Max and the cubs see shadows that look like a flock of birds. They run after them, bumping into each other and rolling on the ground. Laughter fills the forest. They are having so much fun. But then the sun sets and the shadows disappear. "What happened to the shadows?" Max asks.

"It's time for the sun to go to sleep, Max," Mother Tiger says.

"And it's time to go home, but we will see you soon!"

The cubs jump on Max and lick his face goodbye.

Max finds himself back with Mother,
with Hugo licking his face.
"I think Hugo wants to protect you
from the tiger," Mother says with a laugh.

"Thanks, Hugo!" Max says. "But I don't think shadows are scary any more. They can be lots of fun!" He looks at their shadows on the ground and gives a wink to the tiger smiling back at him.

Chrissy Metge

With an extensive background and love of animation it seemed a natural progression to add childrens' author to her list of talents. Max and his Big Imagination was inspired by Chrissy's love for her nephew and the way kids see the world. As a new mother, one of her most favourite things is getting to see all the little things in life, all over again.